KATIE MORAG AND THE NEW PIER

High Farm

The Holiday House

Mrs Bayview's

The Lady Ar

The Redburn Bridge

The Village

THE ISLE of STRUAY

Grannie's

The Mainland

The Jetty

ISLE of STRUAY
SHOP & POST OFFICE

OBAN TIMES
GET YOUR COPY HERE

The Shop & Post Office

ALSO BY MAIRI HEDDERWICK

Katie Morag and the Tiresome Ted
Katie Morag Delivers the Mail
Katie Morag and the Two Grandmothers
Katie Morag and the Big Boy Cousins
Peedie Peebles' Summer or Winter Book

To the old ways – and the new

A Red Fox Book

Published by Random House Children's Books
20 Vauxhall Bridge Road, London SW1V 2SA

A division of Random House UK Ltd
London Melbourne Sydney Auckland
Johannesburg and agencies throughout the world

Copyright © Mairi Hedderwick 1993

3 5 7 9 10 8 6 4

First published in Great Britain by The Bodley Head 1993

Red Fox edition 1994

Printed in Hong Kong

RANDOM HOUSE UK Limited Reg. No. 954009

ISBN 0 09 921161 0

KATIE MORAG AND THE NEW PIER

Mairi Hedderwick

RED FOX

For months workmen had been building a new pier on the Isle of Struay. They were a cheery lot and lived in huts by the shore. They only complained when the weather got too bad to get on with the work; they felt homesick for their families and friends on the mainland.

They looked forward to the day the new pier would be finished. So did the islanders.

Katie Morag was especially excited about the new pier.

"The boat will be able to come to Struay THREE times a week instead of one," said her father, Mr McColl, the shopkeeper.

Mrs McColl, the postmistress, was delighted. She would have lots more mail deliveries to do.

MOUSE TRAPS
12 DOZEN

Post Office

OPEN

XMAS PARTY FUND

Isle of Struay

R.S.P.B. Slide Show Village Hall Wed. Evening

For Sale 6 Lobster Creels

Oban Times Buy your Copy HERE

ISLE OF STRUAY

"Grandma Mainland will be able to come more often," said Neilly Beag.
"And she will be able to get away quicker," said Grannie Island, who was not very sure about the new pier but saw that it had some advantages.

But for the most part Grannie Island was pessimistic.

"The old ways will be forgotten," she frowned. "The place will get too busy; there will be no more jaunts out in the ferryboat to the big boat in the Bay."

Grannie Island often manned the ferryboat on the days that the ferryman was ill or on holiday. "I'll miss that. And so will you, Katie Morag. And what will the ferryman do for a living?" Katie Morag hadn't thought about all that.

In the village people were saying it was time the old ways changed. They started to paint their windows and gates bright colours and tidy their gardens. Mrs Baxter said she was going to open up a Craft Shop. The Lady Artist, of course, was already making interesting things to sell in it.

On the other side of the Bay Mr MacMaster, the farmer, was very pleased. "I'll be able to send off eggs, milk and cheese to the mainland THREE times a week!"

"Ach well," sighed the ferryman, "I suppose I'll soon be redundant."

"What does that mean?" asked Katie Morag.

"No longer wanted," replied the ferryman as he and Katie Morag walked along the shore. Katie Morag nearly tripped over a large, blue, neatly coiled rope on the tideline.

"Finders keepers," said the ferryman. "That's the rule of the sea when something is washed up by the tide".

"Oh no – I'll give it to the ferryboat," declared Katie Morag.

"Have you been having chocolate cake again?" asked Mrs McColl crossly, as Katie Morag toyed with her tea that night. She had, but it wasn't the cake that was making Katie Morag sad. She tried to tell Mr and Mrs McColl all about the ferryman but her parents were not listening.

"The pier will be finished by the spring, weather permitting," said Mrs McColl looking at the calendar.

Spring came but it did not come alone. It was accompanied by fearsome storms. One especially wet and windy day the foreman on the pier told the men to tie down the equipment and stop work. It was boring sitting in the huts waiting for the wild weather to end, so the workmen visited the islanders, and sat by their cosy fires and told stories about life on the mainland.

Jimmy and George were in the McColls' kitchen when the foreman burst in.
"The huts are floating out to sea!" he shouted.

Everyone rushed to the door and sure enough there was the new pier awash, but not a hut in sight save one that bobbed and bucked in the Bay. The rest had all sunk.

There was something else bobbing in the Bay. It was the ferryboat! Katie Morag could just make out the ferryman throwing a rope over the handle of the hut door. But as Grannie Island steered the ferryboat alongside, a huge wave lifted the rope off the handle and the hut started to drift out to sea again.

"Use my rope!" shouted Katie Morag at the top of her voice.

Grannie Island revved the boat close to the hut again and as she circled round it so went the strong blue rope.

Everyone cheered as the ferryboat towed the hut to the shore.

"What seamanship!" said the workmen. "What a rope!" said the ferryman, smiling at Katie Morag as he stepped out of the boat.

TOURIST INFORMATION

YOU ARE HERE

old pier
new pier
Island of Struay

"You can't sleep in that!" said the islanders as sodden mattresses and broken bits of furniture fell out of the hut door.

"You will just have to stay with us until the new pier is finished."

"Great!" thought Katie Morag. "Mainland stories every night!"

Next morning the storm had subsided and the men went back to work. The foreman said the ferryman could keep the hut for fire wood. He and the men thought it was just fine staying in the islanders' homes – much more comfortable than the huts.

Each workman boasted that his lodgings were the best but everyone had to agree that the ferryman's wife's chocolate cake was quite the most fabbydoo.

It was Easter and the new pier was finally completed. The boat came alongside laden with important people and visitors. And there was Grandma Mainland! The workmen shook hands with the islanders and said they would be back for their holidays. Nearly everyone wanted to book in at the ferryman's house and Katie Morag knew why.

"That's it, then," sighed Grannie Island as hordes of visitors meandered towards the village. "The end of the ferryboat and the old ways."

For Sale

Katie
Morag
Recipes

Menu

"No, it is not!" said Katie Morag taking her two grandmothers over to the ferryman's house. The hut was transformed: inside, a counter displayed several chocolate cakes and pots of tea. Grandma Mainland was first in the queue.

"After the visitors have had their tea, you and I and Katie Morag can take them out for a jaunt in the ferryboat, Grannie Island," suggested the ferryman.

"And you can tell them all about the old ways," said Katie Morag. Grannie Island smiled. The new pier was not going to be such a bad thing after all.

Some bestselling Red Fox picture books

THE BIG ALFIE AND ANNIE ROSE STORYBOOK
by Shirley Hughes
OLD BEAR
by Jane Hissey
OI! GET OFF OUR TRAIN
by John Burningham
DON'T DO THAT!
by Tony Ross
NOT NOW, BERNARD
by David McKee
ALL JOIN IN
by Quentin Blake
THE WHALES' SONG
by Gary Blythe and Dyan Sheldon
JESUS' CHRISTMAS PARTY
by Nicholas Allan
THE PATCHWORK CAT
by Nicola Bayley and William Mayne
MATILDA
by Hilaire Belloc and Posy Simmonds
WILLY AND HUGH
by Anthony Browne
THE WINTER HEDGEHOG
by Ann and Reg Cartwright
A DARK, DARK TALE
by Ruth Brown
HARRY, THE DIRTY DOG
by Gene Zion and Margaret Bloy Graham
DR XARGLE'S BOOK OF EARTHLETS
by Jeanne Willis and Tony Ross
WHERE'S THE BABY?
by Pat Hutchins